Every new generation of children is enthralled by the famous stories in our Well-loved Tales series. Younger ones love to have the story read to them. Older children will enjoy the exciting stories in an easy-to-read text.

Published by Ladybird Books Ltd Loughborough Leicestershire UK
Ladybird Books Inc Lewiston Maine 04240 USA

The Snow Queen

retold for easy reading
by JOAN COLLINS
illustrated by KATHIE LAYFIELD

Ladybird Books

The Magic Mirror

Once there was a wicked magician who made a wonderful magic mirror. It turned everything it showed into something ugly.

Beautiful green fields looked like cooked cabbage. Pretty girls' faces were covered with spots. Even your best friend looked horrid. There was something wrong about everything the mirror showed.

Some mischievous goblins thought it was funny. They stole the big mirror and flew up into the sky with it. But it slipped out of their hands and broke into a thousand pieces.

The pieces fell to earth, where people picked them up and looked through them. Some were as big as window-panes, but some were tiny splinters. These stabbed into people's hearts so that they could not feel love or kindness any more. If a speck of mirror glass got into your eye, you saw everything crooked.

Two Children

Down in the city lived a boy and
a girl. Their names were Kay and Gerda,
and they were poor, but very happy.

They lived opposite to each other in the top
floor attics of two tall houses. The roofs were so
close together that the children could climb
across to each other's houses to play.

Kay and Gerda had a little window-box each,
instead of a proper garden. They had planted
two lovely rose trees, which made a flowering
arch between the two windows.

The children could sit under it in the summer and read their books. Sometimes Grandmother told them stories.

In the winter the snowflakes fell, like feathers from the sky, and the wind howled. The children could not play outside, so Grandmother told them tales of the Snow Queen.

"She is the biggest snowflake of all," said Grandmother, "and she flies in the centre of the snowstorm.

"When the wind dies, she goes up into the black clouds. But on winter nights, she flies through the streets and looks in at the windows.

"When she has gone, they are covered with ice flowers."

"Yes, we've seen them!" cried Kay.

"Could she get in here?" asked Gerda timidly.

"Don't worry!" said Kay. "If she does, I'll put her on the stove and she'll melt!"

Sometimes the children would heat pennies on the hot stove, and press them against the frozen window-panes to make peep-holes to look through.

One night Kay was looking out through his peep-hole. He saw a huge snowflake settle on the edge of the window-box. It grew and grew into a wonderful white-coloured woman. She was dressed in a cloak of star-shaped snowflakes and her eyes glittered like icy diamonds.

She beckoned to Kay, but he was afraid and ran back into the room. As she flew away, her shadow passed over the window like a great white bird.

Next day, when Kay and Gerda were playing in the snow, Kay suddenly gave a cry.

"Something went into my eye!" he said. "And I felt a sharp pain in my heart!"

Some pieces of the magic mirror had fallen on Kay.

He turned and kicked over the snowman

Gerda had been building so carefully, and she began to cry.

"Shut up, cry-baby!" said Kay, spitefully.

"Stop fussing, you silly old woman!" he said to Grandmother, who came to see what was the matter.

Kay did not want to play with Gerda any more. He ran out into the street with his wooden sledge, to play in the snow.

A big white sleigh came past, drawn by a swift horse. The driver had a white hooded cloak. Kay could not see the face. Kay fastened his sledge to the back, to get a free ride. The horse went faster than the wind and they were soon in the countryside.

Then they stopped and the driver turned round. It was the Snow Queen!

"You must be cold, little Kay!" she said, in an icy tinkling voice. "Come inside my coat!"

Kay snuggled into it. It was like lying in a deep snowdrift.

The Snow Queen gave him a cold kiss on the forehead. It made Kay forget all about Gerda and his home, as he fell under her spell.

The sledge raced on, high up above the clouds, towards the Snow Queen's palace in the frozen north.

Down below, the cold wind lashed the fields and forests like a whip. Wolves howled and ravens croaked. The huge bright moon came out, and Kay went to sleep, curled up at the Snow Queen's feet.

The Enchanted Flower Garden

Kay had forgotten Gerda, but she did not forget him. She put on her new red shoes and went to look for him. But nobody had seen Kay.

At last Gerda came to a lovely cherry orchard on a river bank. She saw a little house with a thatched roof and windows of yellow, blue and red glass.

An old lady came to the door. She wore a wonderful hat, decorated with bright painted

flowers, and she carried a crooked stick.

Gerda said, "Have you seen Kay?"

"No," said the lady. "But why don't you come in and have some of my cherries?"

While Gerda ate cherries from a crystal bowl, the old lady combed her hair with a golden comb. She was a witch but quite a nice one. She wanted to keep Gerda to be her little girl and live with her always.

The witch had an enchanted garden where it was always summer. Every flower you could think of grew in it, including some lovely roses.

The witch knew that if Gerda saw them, the roses would remind her of Kay. So she thumped with her stick and the rose trees disappeared under the ground.

But the witch had forgotten she had a red rose

painted on her hat. One day Gerda saw it and remembered about Kay.

So she ran away from the old witch and the beautiful garden, where it was always summer. In the world outside, it was autumn.

The yellow leaves were falling, and it was cold.

"Oh, dear!" said Gerda. "What a lot of time I have wasted!"

The Prince and Princess

Gerda struggled on through the snow, for soon it was winter again.

Suddenly she saw a big black crow, which flapped its wings and cawed at her. "What are you doing, little girl, all alone in the snow?"

"I'm looking for Kay," said Gerda. "Have you seen him?"

"Caw, caw! Hum, haw!" croaked the crow hoarsely. "Is he a boy with bright eyes like yours, and golden hair?"

"Yes! Yes!" cried Gerda, and she gave the crow a kiss on his shiny beak.

"Caw! Caw! Wait a bit!" said the crow. "The boy I'm talking about has just married our princess. He's a poor boy who walked up to the palace one day, and the princess fell in love with him."

"That must be Kay," said Gerda. "Everybody loves him. Won't you take me to him?"

"My wife works at the palace," said the crow.
"She will smuggle us into the royal bedroom."

The two birds took Gerda up the back stairs of
the palace, into a wonderful room. The prince

and princess lay asleep in two beds, the shape of lilies. The princess's bed was white, and the prince's bed was red.

Gerda peeped over the edge of the red bed, and the prince woke up. He was a handsome little boy, but he was not Kay!

Gerda was so disappointed she began to cry,

and then the princess woke up too.

When they heard her story, they gave Gerda a dress of silk and velvet, some fur boots and a big warm muff. They lent her a golden coach, with a coachman to drive it, and four white horses. It was filled with sweets and fruit to eat on the journey.

The crows flew to the top of the tallest tree to wave goodbye to Gerda. She promised to come back and see them all when she had found Kay.

The Robber Girl

The golden coach drove on through a great dark forest where robbers were hiding. When they saw it flash past, they rushed out of the trees, shouting "Gold! Gold!"

They killed the coachman and grabbed the horses. Then they dragged Gerda out of the coach.

"She's lovely and plump! I'll eat her for breakfast!" cried a fat robber woman with bushy eyebrows and a beard on her chin.

But her little daughter, who was riding on her mother's back, gave the woman a great bite on her ear. She was a naughty, wild child.

"I want her to play with!" said the Robber Girl. "She must give me her dress and her muff and sleep in my bed!"

And she gave her mother another bite. She was a very strong little girl, with black hair, white

teeth and brown skin, and she always got her
own way.

She told Gerda, "You will be quite safe, if you
do everything I tell you." They drove off
together in the coach to the robbers' castle.

The castle was a ruin, with broken windows and holes in the walls. Ugly black birds flew around it and huge fierce dogs ran about the courtyard. A smoky fire was burning in the middle of the great hall, and some robbers snored round the table. Rabbits and hares were being roasted on spits, for the robbers' supper.

The Robber Girl dragged Gerda over to one

end of the hall, to show her her pets. These were a flock of woodpigeons and doves perched up on the beams. A reindeer was tied up next to her bed.

"He would run away if I didn't tie him up!" she laughed, and tickled his furry throat with her sharp knife.

When they went to bed, under a pile of furs, Gerda told her story. The Robber Girl listened, but soon went to sleep, and snored.

One of the woodpigeons, who had overheard, spoke to Gerda.

"We have seen little Kay in the Snow Queen's sleigh! Coo, coo!"

"What are you saying?" cried Gerda. "Where was the Snow Queen going?"

"Coo, coo! Ask the reindeer!" said the pigeon.

"Oh, yes, the Snow Queen lives in my country," nodded the reindeer.

"Where is that?"

"It is a lovely place called Lapland, covered

with snow and ice. You can run for miles over the frozen plains," said the reindeer, his eyes shining. "She has a summer palace there. Her winter palace is near the North Pole."

"Keep quiet or I'll tickle you with my knife!" said the little Robber Girl sleepily.

In the morning Gerda told the Robber Girl
what the woodpigeon had said.

"The reindeer shall take you to find Kay," the
Robber Girl decided. She gave Gerda back her
fur boots, but kept the muff. Instead she gave
Gerda a huge pair of woolly gloves. She tied her
on the reindeer's back, so that she would not fall
off.

"Here is a loaf of bread and some ham, so you will not be hungry on the way! Now, be off with you, before I change my mind!" she said fiercely.

Gerda and the reindeer set off across the snowy countryside. Wolves howled and ravens croaked and the Northern Lights were flashing in the sky.

As they went further north, it grew colder and colder. They had eaten all the bread and ham when at last they came to Lapland.

The Lapp Woman
and the Finnish Woman

They stopped near a little cottage with a low roof. It was very dark and smelly inside. A greasy-faced old Lapp woman was cooking fish over an oil lamp.

They asked her the way to the Snow Queen's palace. "Oh, you poor souls!" cried the old woman.

"You have more than a hundred miles to go! I had better give you a letter to the Finnish Woman who lives up there. She knows more about it than I do! Now, what can I write on? I haven't any paper."

So she took a dried codfish. "This will do nicely," she said, and scratched a few words on the skin.

So off they set again. The Northern Lights still flashed and flickered in the sky. They were the Snow Queen's fireworks.

When they got to the Finnish Woman's house, they had to knock on the chimney. They could not see the door, it was so small and low.

Inside, it was so hot and steamy the fat Finnish Woman was walking about with hardly any clothes on. Gerda had to take off her boots and gloves.

The Finnish Woman read the letter and then put the dried codfish in the pot to cook. She never wasted anything!

"Please help us!" said the reindeer. "We
know you are a very wise woman and know all
sorts of magic spells."

"Little Kay is in the Snow Queen's palace,"
said the Finnish Woman, "but he likes it there.
That is because he has a piece of glass in his heart
and some dust in his eye, from the Magic Mirror.
He has forgotten Gerda and his old home."

"Can't you give Gerda a magic spell to cure him?" asked the reindeer.

"Gerda already has her own sort of magic," said the Finnish Woman. "Look how all the birds, animals and humans have helped her. She can get into the Snow Queen's palace herself and rescue Kay, because she has the magic power of love.

"All you have to do, reindeer, is to carry Gerda to the edge of the Snow Queen's garden. Put her down by the big bush with red berries on it, and leave her there."

And she began to eat her piece of codfish. The reindeer did as he was told, so quickly that

Gerda had no time to put on her boots and gloves. The reindeer licked her face with his rough tongue, and tears ran down his nose. Then he turned round and scampered off.

There was poor Gerda in the snow, with bare
feet. She ran towards the Snow Queen's palace.
An army of ugly shaped snowflakes was coming
towards her. They were the Snow Queen's
soldiers. Some were like hedgehogs, some like
small bears, some like bunches of snakes. They
were all evil.

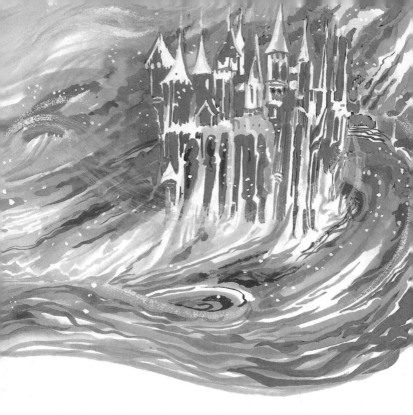

Gerda did not know what to do. She said a little prayer. Her breath came out of her mouth like white mist. It shaped itself into shining snowflakes, like little white angels, who lined up to protect her. The ugly snowflakes vanished, and she could go safely on. She felt quite warm all of a sudden and she was no longer frightened.

What happened in the Snow Queen's palace afterwards

Kay had no idea Gerda was outside. The palace was a huge, empty place, made out of piled up snowdrifts. The windows and doors were holes blown by the biting wind. There were hundreds of halls, opening out of each other, some many miles long.

They were all bitterly cold and lighted by the regular flashing of the Northern Lights. No one had ever held a party in this palace – not even a dance for polar bears!

In the centre of the largest hall was the Snow Queen sitting on her throne, in the middle of a frozen lake of ice. It had cracked into a thousand pieces.

When Gerda found her way into the palace, the Snow Queen had gone. She saw Kay sitting on the steps of the throne, shivering. He was blue with cold but could not feel it, for the Snow Queen had turned his heart to a lump of ice.

He sat playing with pieces of ice and trying to make them into a word. If he could make them spell ETERNITY, the Snow Queen had said she would let him go home. But he had never been able to do it. Gerda ran up to him and put her arms around him.

But Kay was stiff and cold and did not know her. Gerda began to cry. Her warm loving tears ran down Kay's face and on to his chest. The ice in his heart melted and the splinter of glass came out!

Then Kay began to cry too, and the glass dust in his eye was washed away.

When the children looked down, the pieces of ice were dancing about. Then they spelled out a word – ETERNITY!

Kay was free!

"How cold and empty this place is!" he said. "How long have I been here?"

Gerda kissed his face. The pink came back into his cheeks. His eyes shone. Hand in hand, the two children ran out of the icy palace, over the snow, to the bush with red berries.

The reindeer was waiting for them. He whisked them away to the house of the Finnish Woman. There they got warm again and had something to eat.

Then they went to the Lapp Woman's home. She had made them new clothes and lent them her sledge for the rest of the journey.

Winter was left far behind, and the sun came out.

Gerda and Kay found their way back to their own rooftop homes in the city. Grandmother was sitting, reading her Bible, in her old place.

Gerda and Kay were almost grown up now, but they felt as happy again as little children, as they ran together up the attic stairs.